# GHOST

## A NOVELLA

CRYSTAL DANIELS

SANDY ALVAREZ

Vengeance.

It rots, eating at my insides, seeking retribution.

~ Ghost

1

—————

# GHOST

I close my eyes, listening to the sounds of nature surrounding me. The squirrels scamper across the tree branches, and geese honk as they fly in formation above the open meadow. I open my eyes and breathe in the dewy air, which smells of pine, oak, and moss. I scan the open field beyond the tree line, taking in the light gray mist blanketing the grassy area as I sit in silence.

Silence. It can be your greatest adversary and your worst enemy.

I'm a loner, and over the years, I've grown to like my life the way it is. I answer to no one. Keeping myself closed off from the world can sometimes be a heavy weight pressing on my chest. Still, the hurt of loneliness is far less painful than allowing yourself to love and then losing it all.

Solitude is where I find refuge. I live off the grid—away from people, in the middle of the woods, inside a small cabin—where I survive off what the land provides. My life is simple, and I prefer it this way.

I spot movement and watch a large buck slowly make its way out into the clearing. I'm encapsulated in the silence and by the steady rhythm of my heart beating while staring at the young buck through the rifle's scope. The deer raises his head, and from his mouth, blades of grass fall while he chews. His instinct keeps him tuned in to his surroundings, always looking for danger. The six-point antlers on top of his head span wider than his shoulders. I admire the majestic creature for a moment longer before pulling the trigger.

Another successful kill.

A calm breath leaves my body.

I rise from my seat attached to a sturdy oak tree where I'm hidden several feet above the ground. I sling my rifle over my shoulder and descend the ladder to the forest floor. I make my way to my kill and kneel. "Thank you," I murmur, knowing his life will now sustain mine. Every life has a purpose.

Just like *she* had a purpose.

In an instant, I'm having a flashback and find myself swimming in the past, drowning in memories of her.

*Four years ago*

*My wife looks over her shoulder at me while pouring freshly harvested honey into a sanitized mason jar. Her bottom lip pushes out in a pout. "Do you have to go?"*

*"It's only two weeks." I stroll across the kitchen, and Amber catches a drop of honey on her finger and turns to face me.*

*"Taste?" she offers, and I lean in and suck the honey off her fingertip. The sweetness explodes in my mouth while I lose myself in her sapphire-blue eyes. "Good?" She smiles, pulling her finger away.*

*"Not as sweet as you." I bury my face in the crook of her neck, breathing in the scent of honey and wildflowers and thinking how lucky I am.*

*"It's not fair." Amber moans as my lips linger against her skin.*

*"It's my job."*

*She sighs. "I know, but we said 'I do' three days ago. Can't they get someone else to go after the bad guys?"*

*"I'm sorry." Reaching down, I take her delicate hand in mine, lacing our fingers together. The gold and diamond on her ring finger catches the sun just right, making it sparkle. Nestled beside the engagement ring I gave her nearly a year ago is the gold band I placed on her finger last week. I kiss her knuckles. "I can't exactly call in sick or ask a brother to cover for me, babe."*

*"I know." She becomes even more solemn. "It's just... I don't feel good about you leaving this time, Foster." Her free hand lifts, and she rests her palm against my chest over my heart. "I can't shake the feeling that I may never see you again once you leave."*

*"There's always a chance I may not return, honey. You know that." I hate leaving her with worry. I glance at the honeybee clock on the kitchen wall, then look down at my new wife. "I have to go." Leaving loved ones is one of the hardest parts of being married to a military man. "I'll be home soon."*

*"Promise?" She smiles, blinking away tears in her eyes.*

*"I love you, Mrs. McMullan." I press my lips against hers and feel her smiling against them.*

I force myself back into the present, dragging my mind from the pain gripping my insides. Amber had a premonition, and I discarded it as if it were nothing, because tomorrow is never a guarantee when embarking on dangerous missions. I left that day not knowing it would be the last time I'd see the light in her eyes and feel happiness in my heart.

I'm a military man who transitioned into mercenary work. My missions usually revolve around human traffickers, and that operation was no different from before. I met a new unit and worked alongside Riggs and his team, which consisted of five others. On paper and in the field, we accomplished another successful mission. We saved the lives of two dozen young women who finally reunited with their loved ones.

*You reap what you sow.*

Because of my actions, the woman I loved was dead. A crime lord with a vendetta obtained the identities of a few men in my unit, and he set out to kill us all.

Carlito Sanchez was responsible for one of the largest trafficking rings in the States, and I was the one to put a bullet in his head. His father, Angel Sanchez, put a price on our heads and wanted every man on his list executed. Three of my brothers died at the hands of Sanchez's hired hitmen.

I wasn't home when the hitman found my property and made his way into my home, but Amber was. She died when it should have been my life taken. And on a rainy day, as I watched my wife's white casket, covered in wildflowers, lower into the cold ground, a part of me died too.

I had a new mission: kill the sons of bitches responsible for the death of my wife, starting with Angel Sanchez.

Two months later, I would get my first taste of vengeance after learning the location of Sanchez's compound in western Massachusetts. It was also my first-time meeting Salem and his men.

Now, I let my mind take me back to that day.

*I blink a few times, refocusing my eyes, which burn from lack of sleep. I gaze through the binoculars for a moment longer, then let out a heavy sigh and place the equipment back into my pack.*

*I've sat in this dilapidated house across from Sanchez's property since before the break of dawn, watching and waiting for the right time to make my move. The old home smells of mold and vermin excrement. Above my head, the night sky is visible due to the collapsed roof. I turn my attention to a rustling noise to see a rat snake slithering across the dirt and debris on the floor. Knowing he's harmless, I reach over, pull a snack from my bag, rip open another protein bar, then chow down on my dinner.*

*I turn my attention to the substantially large, picture-perfect white farmhouse-style home. From the outside, you would never suspect a ruthless criminal resides there, living what looks to be an everyday, carefree life with a wife and two young daughters. How can the bastard watch his kids grow and sleep at night knowing he's why many young women will never see their families again? It makes me sick to my stomach, and my gut churns with disgust. Several yards away from the main home is a smaller guest house where I've watched Sanchez and a couple of his men spend most of the day. I refocus my anger. Killing Sanchez tonight is the first step toward vindicating my wife.*

*The temperature outside changes, followed by the roll of thunder off in the distance. I look back at the main house, where most lights are off. With it being nearly 2:00 a.m., I'm confident the people inside are sound asleep. I ready myself and stand just as the first drops of rain fall from the sky. The heavy rain pelts at my back and quickly begins soaking my clothes as I trek over the tree-lined landscape leading toward my destination. The front porch light is on but dim. Almost to the side of the guest house, I see the screen door swing open, and one of the two men who's always with Sanchez, steps outside. I drop to my belly, making myself unseen. The moment the man walks to the darker side of the porch, turns his back, and shields himself from the wind to light a cigarette, I make my move.*

*The storm intensifies. Thunder and lightning are the perfect cloaks as I pull a blade from the sheath strapped against my thigh and hop onto the porch. Sanchez's man never sees me coming. I cover his mouth with one hand, plunge the serrated hunting knife into his neck, then swiftly drag his heavy weight backward off the side of the porch. I rip the blade from his neck and restrain the man as he fights to break free. His strength quickly fades as life bleeds from his body. Once his body* goes lax, I release my hold, letting him fall to the soggy ground at my feet.

I stand there momentarily, allowing the rain to wash his blood from my hand and the blade I'm holding.

"Joe." I hear the screen door slam shut, and press against the side of the house, then look down at the man, lying face down a few feet away. Little does the other guy know Joe is dead. Heavy footsteps become louder, echoing off the wooden porch planks. "Yo, dipshit. Boss says it's time to go!" the guy shouts as lightning flashes across the sky, which allows him to spot his dead friend. "What the—"

The unlucky son of a bitch doesn't get to finish his shocked words as I reach out and yank him off the porch to the ground. I drive the knife's blade into the man's side, but it doesn't instantly affect him. Instead, the bastard knees me in the balls, which gives him enough opportunity to roll. Now his heavy ass is on top of me, with one meaty hand pressed against my neck and the other going for the weapon holstered at his side. Like his buddy before him, I bury my blade in the side of his neck and then rip it out. The big bastard falls backward, holding the gaping wound and gasping for air. I get to my feet. With no time to waste, I wipe and sheath my weapon and replace it with my handgun. Leaving Sanchez's second man to die, I stroll onto the porch and open the screen door. Inside, I find the man lounging on an oversized brown leather chair, with a cigar resting between his two fingers while holding a glass of whiskey. He stares at me, unfazed by the gun I have pointed in his direction.

"Who the fuck are you?" he growls, showing no fear.

"The man who killed your son." Hate grows in Sanchez's eyes at my declaration, and his nostrils flare. I continue to make my way across the room, water dripping from my soaked clothes onto the wood floor. "You had to have known this day would come."

Sanchez glares at me. "Ah, yes. I remember you. Your woman's life was a small price for killing my boy." He lifts his chin with an air of *defiance and righteousness. He leans further back into his seat. "You'll be dead before you can pull the trigger." He smirks.*

*"Your men are dead," I tell him, wiping the condescending smile from his face. The realization that he's about to die flashes across his smug face.*

*"Go to hell," he sneers.*

*"I'm already there, motherfucker." Thunder rattles the windows of the house as I pull the trigger, then the power goes out.*

*"You just cost me a lot of money." The disembodied voice has me ready to kill again. A cigarette tip glows in the darkness, giving me a glimpse of the man behind the deep voice.*

*I aim my weapon at him. "I have no problem adding to tonight's body count."*

*He blows out a puff of smoke. "I believe it." He pauses, and the lights flicker back on. Several more men enter the room from various corners of the house. "But, if I wanted to stop you from killin' my paycheck, I would have already done it." He cocks his head like we're having a casual conversation. "My men and I watched you take out both men outside, and then I overheard why you were here to kill Sanchez." The man, wearing a biker cut with the name Salem, waits to see if I will speak. I choose to keep quiet. My business here is none of his concern, and I sure as shit don't feel like talking it out with a fucking stranger. "A man's business is his own. Your retribution far outweighed the price on the sick bastard's head."*

*Sensing no threat from him and his men, I holster my weapon, take one final look at Sanchez's lifeless body, then turn and walk out the door.*

It wouldn't be the last time I ran into Salem and the men of Fallen Ravens MC. Over time we became allies.

**2**

# BEATRIX

Do you ever dream about abandoning your current life and starting over somewhere else, hundreds of miles away, where nobody knows you? I do. I think about doing that every day. I honestly don't know what's holding me back. I have no ties to Boston, no real roots. I lost the only thing anchoring me to this place when Dad died last year. Thinking about my father and how much I miss him causes a bone-chilling ache to settle in my chest, making it hard to breathe.

Taking a deep breath, I rub my thumb over the spot on my right wrist where a tattoo of a small bumblebee sits. Looking at the bumblebee grounds me, and I can't help smiling. My father gave me the name Beatrix Lou Owens. My dad's name was Lou, and though not many fathers would name their daughter after them, I never minded. I loved my dad, and I am proud to carry his name.

To most people, I'm Bea, but I was always Bumble Bea to my dad. I was twelve when I learned that my mother had abandoned me. Dad said he and my mom didn't know each other well. She was someone he'd gone on a couple of dates with, and then one

8

day, he never heard from her again. Nine months later, he got a phone call from her saying she was in the hospital and she'd just had his baby. Dad told me he'd been thrown for a loop at the news but didn't question my mom or think twice about dropping everything and hightailing it to the hospital to be by her side. My mom's name was Lynn, and he stayed in that hospital room for two days. He hung on every word the doctors said and didn't miss a detail when the nurses explained feedings and how to change my diaper. Dad said he fell in love when the nurse placed me in his arms. He told me Lynn had agreed to come to live with him even though he only had a one-bedroom apartment.

Dad had just started a new construction job, but he was determined to do whatever it took to support the three of us. When Mom was scheduled for discharge from the hospital, my dad came to the hospital straight from work with a brand-new car seat in hand to find my mom had left. It was the nurses who had to break the news. That was the day we became Lou and Bea. Just him and me. It was us against the world. And because I'd never known my mother, I never felt I was missing out on anything. My father adored me, and even though, at times, we didn't have much, I never wanted for anything.

I've lived in Boston my whole life. Dad and I stayed in that tiny one-bedroom apartment until I was five, and then we moved into a two-bedroom, one-bath house in a nice neighborhood. He worked so hard for that house, and he was so proud. I still live here to this day. My home holds so many good memories. It's probably the only thing keeping me in Boston. When my dad got sick with pancreatic cancer, he told me to sell the house and move out of the city as I've always wanted. He knew I struggled with the idea because of how much our home meant to me, but he said our memories are not rooted in things or places but our hearts. Just because I move away doesn't mean I move on from the life we shared, and it doesn't mean I forget.

I don't even know what I want to do with the rest of my life. We got Dad's diagnosis when I was twenty-one, and I had to drop out of college to get a full-time job to help support him. He had fought me on it, but dropping out was no sacrifice. He needed me, and I was going to be there for him. One of Dad's good friends offered me a job at his bar, so I took it. Mr. Sullivan has always been like an uncle to me. I still work at Sullivan's to this day.

"Hey, Bea. I didn't know you were on tonight," Hadley, one of the other waitresses at Sullivan's, says as she breezes into the break room.

I look down at my dinner that I've barely touched and realize I've spent most of my break in a daze. Standing, I toss my half-eaten sandwich and chips into the trash. "Sullivan called me last minute, because Lane was a no-show again," I tell her.

Hadley shakes her head. "I can't believe he hasn't canned her ass already."

"Yeah, but you know how the old man is. His heart is too soft. And he did promise me I could take Monday off if I came in, giving me a three-day weekend." Which I'm looking forward to. Because of Lane, I haven't had a day off in nine days.

"That will be nice." Hadley smiles. "Any big plans with your time off?"

I huff out a laugh. "Not likely. I have a mountain of laundry to wash, a sink full of dishes, and my grass needed mowing two weeks ago."

"Boring," Hadley sing-songs, then snaps her fingers. "I know. How about you come with me to the East of Addiction concert this weekend? My brother is working security at the venue and snagged me a pair of tickets."

"Hmm."

"Look; just think about it and let me know by Friday night. If you don't come with me, I'll be forced to take my little sister." She scrunches her nose.

I laugh. "Fine, I'll think about it."

Tying an apron around my waist, I make my way behind from the break room and onto the main floor, where I'm assaulted with the smell of beer and chicken wings. I smile over at Sully, behind the bar, then make my way to my section, where one of our regulars is seated. "Evening, Russ." Russ has been coming into Sullivan's at least three times a week for the past year, and he always sits in my section. I'd put Russ in his mid-thirties with brown hair, brown eyes, and glasses. Most days, he wears suits, and I always pegged him as a teacher or an accountant, though I've never asked. Russ keeps to himself. He has never gotten handsy like other men do when they drink too much, and he always orders the same thing.

"Good evening, Beatrix." Russ pushes his wire-rimmed glasses up his nose.

"You want your usual?" I ask.

"Yes."

"No problem. I'll put your order in and be back with your drink."

Turning, I weave through the tables and make my way up to the bar.

"I already put the order in for a cheeseburger and onion rings." Sully sets a bottle of light beer and a bottle of water on my tray.

"Thanks, Sully."

He nods and continues down the bar to tend to the two women sitting down.

"Here ya go, Russ." I set the water and beer down on the table. "Your grub will be out in about five minutes. Can I get you anything else?"

"Thanks, Beatrix."

As the night winds down, my feet are screaming, and my back is aching.

"Hey, Bea. You want to get the door?" My boss jerks his chin toward the last patron, who is now leaving.

"Sure." I shuffle behind the man and offer a smile. "Have a good night." I lock the door and begin clearing the empty bottles and wiping down the tables.

"Was he the last one?" Hadley asks.

"Yup," I call out.

"Oh, thank god." She collapses into one of the booths, and I follow suit and sit down across from her. "You had a rowdy bunch tonight."

"You aren't lying. College kids are the worst. And they don't tip worth a shit."

"Yeah, well, next time I see those little piss-ants in here, I'm tossing them out," Sully grumbles.

The guys Hadley had the displeasure of dealing with tonight sent their food back twice and "accidentally" dropped two beer bottles on the floor. They were too loud and almost got into it with a couple of regulars, men who would have wiped the floor with their butts if Sully hadn't stepped in and defused the situation.

"Those jerks left two dollars and thirty-seven cents in change as a tip for putting up with their sorry asses."

"Are you serious?" I ask, shaking my head.

"We can't all have regulars like Russ." Hadley waggles her eyebrows. "I'm telling you, that man has it bad."

I roll my eyes. "No, he's just a sweet man, not my type."

"You should see how he watches you when he's here. Seriously, it's creepy." She shivers.

If I'm being honest, I have noticed how Russ looks at me, which kind of weirds me out. He gets this intense look on his face.

"You two quit dilly-dallying so we can get out of here," Sully fusses.

"Alright, alright, keep your pants on, Sully," Hadley grumbles.

"Come on." I giggle while pulling on her arm. "Let's finish so we can go home. My feet are killing me."

It's close to 2:00 a.m. when Sullivan, Hadley, and I are trudging through the empty parking lot to our vehicles. My friend tosses a wave over her shoulder, and I wave back. Our boss stops at his truck which is parked right beside my car. "Appreciate you coming in, Bea. You always rescue me when I'm in a bind."

I look at Sullivan and take in his haggard face and sparkling blue eyes. He should have retired five years ago, but this bar is his life. He has two sons. One is in construction, and the other has an excellent job at the bank. Neither are interested in taking it over. I suspect he doesn't have the heart to let it go. He talked about selling the business a few months before my dad passed, but nothing ever came of that notion. I often wonder if he keeps the place because I keep coming to work.

I admitted to Sullivan one day, not long after losing Dad, that I thought about leaving Boston and starting over elsewhere. With my dad gone, this place no longer feels like home. Since my confession, my boss has pushed me to bite the bullet, get out of this city, and start living. The only thing holding me back is fear. I'm afraid of leaving what's familiar and going off into the unknown.

"Anytime." I give him a tired smile. "I'll see you next week, Sully."

"I hope I don't, kid." He climbs into his truck. Sully says those exact words to me every night I leave the bar. After my little confession, he told me he secretly hopes every day is the day he doesn't see me walk into his bar. He said the day I don't show up for work will be the day he knows I've decided to leave and live the life I deserve instead of wasting my days with an older man like him. And every day I walk into that bar to work my shift, I can see the disappointment on his face for a split second.

When I pull up to the house, I cut the engine off and stare

through the cracked windshield. I close my eyes and think back to some of the last words my dad spoke to me.

"Go off and live your life, Bumble Bea. Find what makes you happy. I'll always be with you, no matter where you go."

Shaking those thoughts away, I climb out of my car. I'm just about to my door when the hairs on my arm stand up, and I hear footsteps behind me. Turning, I let out a gasp, and my purse falls to the ground when I see Russ step out of the shadows. "Jesus Christ." I clutch my keys to my chest and take in a lungful of air. It doesn't take a moment for me to come to my senses, and when I do, a ball of dread starts forming in my stomach. Everything about what's happening is setting off alarm bells.

"Sorry. I didn't mean to scare you, Beatrix." He takes another step toward me, and I tense.

"Ru-Russ, what are you doing here? How do you know where I live?"

Russ tilts his head to the side. "I always make sure you get home safe."

"Um...Russ, I'm not sure that's appropriate." My voice shakes. "I think you need to leave."

His demeanor changes. "You should be thanking me for keeping you safe." He takes another step toward me. I retreat, my back hitting the front door to my house. Not wanting to anger him any further, I try a different tactic.

"You're right. I'm sorry. Thank you, Russ, for making sure I got home safe." My shaky hand fiddles with my keys. "Now, if you'll excuse me, I'm exhausted and want to get inside." I twist my body sideways and try to insert my key into the lock while not wanting to take my eyes off him.

"Aren't you going to invite me in?" He becomes more agitated, and my eyes drop to where he's pulling something from his pocket.

"I'm—I'm sorry, but I'm tired. Maybe some other time." There's no denying the fear in my voice. As I turn back to the door, the keys fall from my grasp, and Russ lunges at me.

"No!" is the only word I get out before his cloth-covered hand clamps over my mouth. The last thing I remember before my vision blurs and darkness takes me is the feel of his sweaty forehead against my cheek and his heavy breathing in my ear.

# 3

# GHOST

I glance around the smoke-filled bar and take another sip from the glass of whiskey—the bitter liquor coats my taste buds and sets fire to my throat. Setting the glass on the table, I lift the lit cigarette from the ashtray to my lips. My lungs burn as I hold the nicotine in, only expelling the smoke from my body when my brain tells me I need to breathe. The bar scene usually isn't my thing—too many people. But the low-key bar is the meeting place we agreed on since Laredo contacted me with the information. I keep my eyes trained on the bar's entrance.

A few minutes later, Laredo strolls through the door, scans the room, and finds me at the back, sitting at a corner table. I did the club a favor a short time ago, gathering intel on a rival MC. Just one of many ways I've become involved with the club over the past few years. I'm good at what I do and have an array of resources at my disposal for gathering information on people. Those connections produced nothing in my search for Mejia, where Laredo has stepped in and helped.

Laredo stops by the bar and leans over the counter, speaking to the female bartender before continuing in my direction.

"How's it goin'?" he asks while pulling out a chair, then takes a seat.

"I'm breathing," I say, detached from the world around me and down what remains of my whiskey. "What you got for me?" I'm eager to get my hands on anything he is here to give.

Laredo scrubs his hands over his face and down his beard and leans back, letting out a heavy breath. "Not to piss on your already sour mood, brother, but I just drove an hour after a long ass day to meet you here. I'm going to relax and have a fuckin' beer before diving into business."

I don't respond and only nod with understanding. The man deserves to unwind, after all. A waitress arrives at our table and sits a cold beer in front of Laredo. She smiles at him. "Hey, handsome. I haven't seen your face in here before."

"Not from around here, darlin'." His Texas drawl hooks her instantly.

"Are you a cowboy or something?" she asks.

He grins. "Somethin' like that."

Her eyes linger on Laredo for a moment, then turns her attention toward me. "Hey again, stranger." She notices the empty glass in front of me and reaches across the table. In the process, the waitress's tits, barely contained by the small crop top she's wearing, are in my face, front, and center." She notices my glance downward and gives a flirty smile. "Would you like a refill?"

"I'm good."

She gives off serious fuck-me vibes. "You men need anything, just let me know." She winks, then slowly retreats, sashaying toward the other side of the bar.

Laredo whistles. "Damn, brother. That pretty lady wants a taste of somethin'."

"Not interested," I tell him, and he gives me a *you've got to be out of your fucking mind* look.

He shakes his head. "Shit, if you don't leave here with her

tonight, I just might." He turns in his seat, setting his unwanted attention on me, and downs some of his beer.

We sit in silence for a beat until I can't take him eyeballing me anymore. "Spit it out," I grumble, knowing by the way Laredo's stare is searing a fucking hole through my head that he has something to say.

"I get that you've embraced this lone wolf lifestyle, but have you given any more thought to Salem's offer?" Laredo is referring to becoming a brother and riding with Fallen Ravens MC. I like the club and the brotherhood they offer, but I like my solitude more. At least for now. What Fallen Ravens does and how they operate isn't much different than what I do. They rid the world of unwanted gutter trash for a price. I scrub the palm of my hand down my face and sigh, not knowing if I should turn the club's offer down or stew on it longer.

"I'm not ready to give you an answer." I keep it real with Laredo.

"Fair." He nods. "It's fuckin hard for a man to move forward when he has unfinished business." Laredo reaches into his cut, producing a folded envelope. "Hopefully, this sets you on the path to doing just that." He slides it across the table.

I lean forward, pick the envelope up and open it. Papers inside reveal the alias Russ Blackwell that Mejia has been hiding behind, along with an address and three photographs. The man in these pictures has an altered appearance from the only images I have of Mejia. His hair is shorter and dyed a different color. However, time and effort have done nothing to hide who he is. Behind those brown-colored contacts are the eyes of a murderer. Edges of the paper crinkle as my grip tightens around the edges while staring at the image of my wife's killer.

"You want backup on this one?" Laredo asks.

"No." I push from the table, causing the chair's feet to scrub loudly against the bar's hardwood floor, and I stand. "I owe you." I set my attention on Laredo.

"You don't owe me shit. A word of advice—wisdom—whatever you want to fuckin' call it. Vengeance is a deceitful and bloodthirsty motherfucker, and he'll always want more unless you learn to have the strength to let him go. Don't let him destroy you." His jaw ticks and I can see in his eyes that he connects with what he is saying. "I hope killing the man finally gives you some peace."

His words are a jagged pill to swallow, so, for now, I don't. I need vengeance and his greedy thirst to finish what I started. Not giving Laredo a response, I walk out of the bar to my truck and head home to prepare to mark off the last name on my list.

**4**

# BEATRIX

*"Daddy, I don't think I can do it."*

*"Sure you can. Just hold on to the handlebars and put your feet on the pedals," Daddy says. "Go on, Bea. You got this."*

*Taking a deep breath, I tighten my grip on the handlebars. "You promise not to let go?"*

*"I promise. I won't let go until you're ready."*

*Daddy always keeps his promises, so I know he won't let me fall. "Okay, I'm ready."*

*"Alright, Bea. Feet on the pedals and look straight ahead."*

*Nodding, I kick my feet up and start to pedal with Daddy holding onto the seat behind me.*

*"There you go! Keep pedaling, Bea. Pedal! Pedal! Pedal!" he cheers.*

*I squeal as he runs behind me, still holding on. "Let go, Daddy! Let go!"*

*"Are you sure?" he asks.*

*"Yes! Let go, Daddy!"*

*Daddy lets go and starts jumping up and down. "Go, Bumble Bea! Go!" He claps. "That's my girl!"*

*I start laughing as the warm summer breeze hits my face. "I'm doing it, Daddy!"*

*After pedaling to the end of the street, I push the brakes. Looking over my shoulder, I see him running toward me with the biggest smile.*

*"Did you see me, daddy?"*

*"I saw, Bumble Bea." He scoops me off the bike into a bear hug. Daddy has the best hugs. "I knew you could do it. I'm so proud of you." He kisses my cheek, and his scruffy chin hair tickles, making me giggle. "What do you say? Think you can ride back to the house yourself?"*

*I nod. "Let's do it."*

I wake with a pounding in my head and catapult back to the present. I try to bring my hand up to rub my eyes only to have something cold and heavy around my right wrist stop me. Startled, I quickly sit up, momentarily confused by my surroundings. The ground is hard and cold, like the metal cuffs around my wrists and the chain attached to a wooden post sticking out of the cement floor. "What the..." My heart jackhammers in my chest as I look around the darkened room with a slight chill causing my skin to break out in chill bumps. The smell of mold and dirt permeates the air. Before I know it, I'm on the verge of hyperventilating.

"Hello," I call out. Ignoring the pounding in my head, I climb to my feet and walk a couple of steps, but am stopped abruptly by the chain connecting me to the beam. I start tugging on it and frantically try to free my hands from the metal bands around my wrists. It's no use.

Suddenly, the sound of heavy footfalls above my head causes me to be still. The steps grow closer and louder, followed by the sound of hinges squeaking with the opening and closing of a door. My eyes dart over to a set of stairs, and I watch as a pair of boots appear, then legs, and eventually a face. I suck in a sharp breath.

Suddenly it all comes flooding back. Russ at the bar, him creeping up on me at my house, then a struggle. And suddenly, the man in front of me no longer looks like the sweet shy man I've thought he was for the past year he's been coming into Sullivan's.

"Russ, wh... what's going on?" I pull on the chain again. "Please let me go," I plead.

"You know; I didn't plan this. Not really," he says, stalking across the room. "It's been a while since anyone has caught my interest. Not since my team disappeared," he continues, further confusing me with his rambling. "But then I saw you." He stops and looks at me, his gaze raking me from head to toe. "Sullivan's is not even in my part of town. It was sheer luck that I happened to be there that Saturday night a year ago. I was supposed to meet a friend. He said he found us a new girl but didn't show up. He just up and vanished." Russ shakes his head and gets a faraway look on his face. A moment later, he snaps out of his daze and his attention is back on me, his current expression replaced with one that has the hairs on the back of my neck standing up. An unwelcome sense of fear washes over me. He approaches me, and I shrink away. "It was fate, Beatrix. And now you are mine."

"Get away from me." My voice trembles. "You're crazy. Let me go." I tug on the chain holding me hostage.

His eyes narrow. "You're not going any fucking where." In one quick movement, Russ reaches out and grips a handful of my hair, wrenching me forward.

"Don't touch me!" I scream, and claw at his face. I have a brief sense of satisfaction when I draw blood, which starts dripping down his cheek.

"Fucking bitch," he hisses, his grip on my hair tightening and making me wince, but that doesn't stop the fight in me.

With my adrenaline kicking in, I start to kick and flail in his arms. My elbow connects with his nose, and he loses his grip on my hair, but not before shoving me backward. My back slams against the wooden post, knocking the air from my lungs.

"I see you're going to be a hard one to break," Russ sneers, cupping his hand over his bleeding nose. "That's okay. I'll enjoy hearing you scream while you crumble into pieces." In two strides, he's on me again, taking my head between the palms of his hands just before slamming my head back into the post. I barely register the sharp pain in my skull before the lights go out again.

*"I don't know what I'm going to do without you." I can't stop the tears running down my face as I look down at my dad lying in the hospital bed.*

*Dad pats the side of the bed. "Come here, Bumble Bea."*

*I crawl beside him and put my face into the crook of his neck, inhaling the scent of Old Spice. "I'm sorry, Dad. I'm supposed to be the strong one, yet here you are, comforting me."*

*He chuckles. "That's what parents do. It doesn't matter how old our children get; it's our job."*

*A few minutes ago, I stood by my father's hospital bed and listened to him tell the doctor that he refused further treatment and wanted to live out the rest of his days at home. I'd known this day was coming, but I hadn't thought it would be this soon. Dad got the diagnosis two years ago and has been fighting ever since.*

*"Life is so unfair." I sniffle.*

*"I don't know if I'd say that."*

*I sit up and swipe angrily at my face. "How can you not?"*

*"If life were so unfair, I wouldn't have had the blessing of being your dad. If life were unfair, God wouldn't have given me you." Dad cups my cheek. "I'd say life has been pretty damn good because I have my Bumble Bea."*

*"Dad." I hiccup.*

*"I believe my sole purpose is to be your dad. I was given twenty-one*

*of the best years of my life, and I wouldn't change one second of those twenty-one years for anything. Not for nothing. My greatest achievement is being your father and watching you become the woman you are today. And I can honestly say that I will die a happy man and have no regrets."*

*I throw myself against my dad's chest, and he wraps his arms around me. I don't know how long we lie in that hospital bed together.*

*I must have dozed off. I'm no longer lying in the hospital bed with my father when I open my eyes. Instead, I'm in a basement. But that doesn't seem right because we don't have a basement. I let my eyes roam around until they fall on a lone figure curled into a ball on the floor. I step closer and gasp when I realize what I'm looking at. "Oh my god." I cover my mouth with my hand.*

*"Don't be scared, baby girl."*

*I turn to find my dad. He doesn't look sick at all. He looks healthy, like he did two years ago. "Dad? What's going on? How come you... Why am I..."*

*"No, you're not dead." Dad smiles. "I know you're confused, but I'm here to let you know everything will be okay."*

*I look at my dad, shake my head, then look back at the woman lying on the floor. "What happened? How did I get here?"*

*"Everything has a purpose, Beatrix. I know you don't understand that now and are scared."*

*"Daddy." My voice shakes.*

*"I'm going to need you to be brave, Bumble Bea. For just a little while longer. Can you do that?"*

*I run to my dad and throw my arms around him, finding comfort in the familiar scent of Old Spice. "Can't I come with you?" I ask.*

*Dad kisses the top of my head. "It's not your time, sweetheart."*

*"But—"*

*Dad gently pulls back and looks into my eyes. "Do you remember that time when you were eight, and you swore up and down there was a ghost living in your closet?"*

*I nod.*

*"And remember you slept with me for a month before I could convince you there was no ghost?"*

*I nod again. "Yes. I had a sleepover at Jenny Banks' house, and her mom let us watch the movie Thirteen Ghosts. That movie freaked me out. You had to explain how it was all make-believe, but I was still scared." I look over my shoulder at the figure lying on the floor, then back at my dad again. "Why are you asking me about something that happened when I was eight? I don't understand what's happening."*

*"I know, Bumble Bea. But can you do your old man one last favor?"*

*"Of course. I'd do anything for you, Dad."*

*Dad squeezes my shoulders. "I want you to remember that some ghosts exist, but the ones that exist are there to protect you."*

*"Like you?" I ask.*

*Dad shakes his head. "No. I'm your guardian angel and here to watch over you."*

*"Then what ghost are you talking about?"*

*"You'll see, baby girl. But remember; don't be afraid."*

*"Okay, Daddy. I won't."*

*"That's my girl." He kisses my cheek. "It's time for me to go, and it's time for you to wake up."*

*"I don't want you to go, Dad. I want you to stay with me."*

*"I'll always be with you, Beatrix."*

*"I love you, Daddy."*

*"I love you too, Bumble Bea."*

I blink my eyes to the same pounding in my head and the same smell of dirt and mildew, making me realize I am no longer dreaming but still trapped in a nightmare.

5

———

# GHOST

I look at my watch and fixate on the second hand as it moves. As time ticks away, my thoughts transport me back to the moment I made my first vengeance kill. The satisfaction of pulling the trigger and watching life leave Sanchez's body still resonates. Now, I finally get to end the life of the man who sought to kill me but murdered another. The rage inside me intensifies, vibrating from my core and throughout my body. The hunger to see Mejia dead grows with every breath I take.

I'm jolted to the present as an ominous howling gust moves through the tops of tall oak trees as a northern wind blows. I smell the dampness in the air before hearing rolling thunder in the distance.

I look down once more and note the time. It's nearly noon, and my blood runs so cold it sends a chill down my spine. *Life and its cruel irony.* At this precise time, four years ago, I found out my wife was dead. Murdered at the hands of the man I aim to kill today.

For four years, I have worked alone and sought vengeance, taking my rage and using it to rid the corrupt humans thriving among us. I've brought the damned souls to the smoldering gates

26

of hell and laid their rotting corpses at Satan's feet in the name of justice. All in the attempt to rid the world of evil while I try to outrun my demons, acutely aware I'm slowly digging my grave, filled with the bitter taste of hate and in a constant state of unrest.

Perhaps I'll finally find peace with Mejia's blood on my hands.

I focus my attention back on the house. There has been no activity for hours, and from my surveillance, he is the only person in the home. I rise from my crouched position and check my weapons, then walk out from the tree line and cautiously approach the side of the house. Careful not to rattle the chain-link fence enclosing the backyard, I climb over it and move toward the back door. I crouch on one knee, dig my tools out of my front pocket, and pick the lock. Something moves, causing the leaves of the bush near the porch to rustle. I pause, waiting to see if anything emerges, but nothing appears.

With my gun raised, I slowly turn the handle and open the door, entering a laundry room that leads into the kitchen. The rooms are dark as I make my way through the home. Once I've cleared the first floor, I head for a set of steps leading to the second level of the house. Before ascending the steps, I feel something brush against my ankle, causing me to cast my eyes toward the floor, where I notice a gray kitten at my feet, smaller than my boot. *Where the hell did you come from?* Its presence is a brief distraction before I continue up the stairs.

There's a dim light casting across the hallway and the sound of someone moving and water running coming from the light source's location. My adrenaline kicks into high gear, which heightens my senses, and I keep my weapon raised and approach. As I step to the partially-opened bathroom door, I see his reflection in the mirror above the bathroom sink. There he is, my wife's murderer, washing a bloody cat-like scratch across his right cheek.

"The good for nothin' whore," Mejia hisses. "She's going to be beggin' for death by the time I'm done using her." He spits into the sink and then turns off the water. His face tightens and his movement stills. His eyes lift, looking in the mirror. I step forward, letting him see me emerge from the shadows, and his empty stare locks with mine.

Before he can react, I burst into the bathroom, making him backpedal until the backs of his knees hit the toilet while the barrel end of my gun stays pressed against his eye socket. "Have a seat, motherfucker." I force him to lower his ass onto the toilet. He studies me for a beat before speaking.

"I know you." He grins menacingly. "You're that soldier boy I meant to kill a few years ago." Mejia regards me with amusement. "You cost me a lucrative payday not being where you were supposed to be that day." Then he smirks. "Lucky for me, that sweet woman of yours was good compensation."

Needing to inflict pain but not willing to kill him yet, I grip a handful of his hair, haul him off the toilet, and slam his face against the edge of the ceramic sink bowl several times before standing up and hitting his back against the wall. I wrap my hand around his scrawny neck. Blood runs profusely from his disfigured nose. Being the twisted motherfucker he is, Mejia breathes heavily and laughs through the pain.

"You enjoy the kill just as much as I do." His face reddens. "You are no different from me," he spits as I constrict his airway, intending to take his life with my bare hand.

The adrenaline pumping through my veins barely lets me register the searing heat rippling across my side. I tear my eyes away from the son of a bitch's face and look down to find his hand wrapped around the handle of a blade he sunk into my side.

I absorb the pain radiating through my flesh from the wound he inflicted. The darkness inside me feeds off it. He shoves the blade further into my body as I begin prying open his mouth, forcing the barrel of my gun through his clenching teeth and down his throat. Mejia gags, coughing and gasping for air, but he never breaks his hold on the knife sunk in my side, and his soulless eyes stay locked on mine. I have nothing to say. All I want is for my face to be the last he sees.

I pull the fucking trigger, and just like that, my mission is complete.


I pull the blade from my side, gritting my teeth before dropping the knife to the floor. I snatch a hand towel off the wall hanging by the sink and press it against the wound. Giving one last look at Mejia's lifeless body, I walk out of the bathroom.

Once downstairs, I head for the exit, but meowing causes me to turn. Spotting the fuzzball making the commotion near a slightly ajar door, I holster my weapon, wipe my bloody hand on my pants leg while keeping pressure to my side with the other, and stride over to where the kitten is. "Hey there." I lift the kitten and hold it in front of me, then look around and realize the little guy must have wandered in through the back door. "Was that you outside in the bushes?"

A soft moan coming from the cracked door catches my attention. "Someone down there?" I ask the kitten, who promptly meows as if it understood. With the furball in my hand, I pull open the door leading to the basement and descend into a dimly lit space. On the far side of the room, my eyes stop scanning when I notice a dirty cot on the floor and a young woman lying in the fetal position. "Shit," I hiss and rush toward her. Placing the kitten on the floor, I kneel and run my eyes over her body, which is battered and covered in bruises. I brush her red hair from her face to see it swollen and bruised. "You're the woman he was referring to upstairs." I lift her arm to press my fingers against her wrist, feeling for her pulse. It's steady. That's when I spot the bee tattoo beneath my fingertips. The young woman moans again, and one of her swollen eyes cracks open, locking onto my face.

"Help me," she says in a defeated whisper.

Without giving more thought to the situation, I scoop the woman into my arms, grunting through the pain I'm beginning to feel at my side as my adrenaline wears off. "You're safe now," I tell her, and feel her body relax against my chest. A soft meow has me turning my head, and the kitten stares at me. "Come on." I pick the little guy up, too, and carry the woman and kitten out of the house.

It's a decent trek through the woods back to the location of my truck. On the way, it begins raining, and the three of us are soaked when I finally get to my ride.

I open the passenger door, place the woman in my truck, grab a blanket stuffed behind the seat, and wrap her in it. Using the corner of the blanket, I dry the kitten off and set it beside my passenger before buckling her in and closing the door. Before I climb in behind the steering wheel, I dig through a bag tossed in the bed of my truck and take out a large roll of gauze from the first aid kit. I lift my shirt to inspect the puncture wound on my side, which I pack with gauze to control the bleeding until I get home. Needing something to keep it in place, I dig inside the truck's tool box, pull out a roll of duct tape, then wrap it around my torso to hold the gauze in place. I start the engine and blast the heat to help dry our clothing.

Turning on my seat toward the stranger in my presence, I look her over. Water drips from my hair, rolling down my face as I stare at the young woman. Even covered in bruises, I notice her beauty.

Her teeth chatter from being wet and cold. I reach out, unbuckle her seatbelt, and pull her across the bench seat, placing her body against mine for extra heat. In the process, the furball moves, climbing onto my lap and curling into a tight ball. *What the fuck have I gotten myself into?*

"Thank you," the young woman whispers, her voice soft as she drifts back into an exhausted sleep.

I say nothing. Instead, I look around for my phone and place a call. Usually, I clean up my messes, leaving no traces of my presence.

"What's up?" Salem says, his voice relaxed.

"I need a favor."

"I'm all ears, brother," Salem says, and I fill him in on needing assistance cleaning the scene. Salem doesn't needle me for more information than I'm giving. "I'll be in touch." Then he ends the call.

I give the woman beside me one final look, then drive off down the dirt road. Silence drowns the truck's cab for a considerable time until I stop at the fork in the road. One way leads toward town, where the nearest hospital is. The other direction takes me home. *Why in the hell am I hesitating?* I glance down at the woman nestled at my side. She needs to see a doctor. I watch the steadiness of her breaths.

I grip the steering wheel. "Hey." I drop a hand and touched her cheek. She rouses, but not much. "Got anyone lookin' for ya?"

"Probably not," she says with a pang of great sadness in her tone.

"What's your name?"

"Bea." She takes a shivered breath. "Who are you?" Her voice drifts at the end of her question.

"Ghost."

"Ghost," she whispers.

I can't explain why, but I decide to take her home.


An hour later, I'm pulling up to my cabin. With Bea and the kitten in my arms, I ignore my discomfort and carry them inside. I take her straight to my room and lay her down on the bed. She moans as I get the still-damp clothing off her body and further assess her injuries. "Sorry," I say, after causing her to flinch when pressing against her ribcage. "Nothing feels broken." I strip her down to her bra and panties, tuck a pillow beneath her head, her hair still dampened from the rain, then cover her with a couple of blankets. I leave the room for a second, going to the kitchen and returning with a glass of water and pain medication, which I break in half and help Bea sit up.

"Take this." I hold the medicine and water out, but she hesitates. "It's for the pain. I know it's hard for you to trust a man after what you've been through, but I promise you're safe with me, Bea." I do my best to reassure her. With shaky hands, she takes the pill, slips it past her swollen lips, and drinks the water. I walk away again into the bathroom and wet a washcloth with warm water, then ring it out. I sit on the bed and wipe the dried blood and dirt from Bea's bruised face. Anger churns in my gut as I think about Mejia laying hands on her. I'd kill him all over again if given a chance.

After I help her rest back against the pillow again, I move to leave. She needs her rest, and I need to sort out the gamut of thoughts and emotions swirling inside my head.

Bea reaches out, taking hold of my hand. "Stay with me." Electricity shoots through my body at her touch. I don't understand why I choose to stay, but I do.


After Bea falls into a deep, medicated sleep, I leave her side, strip out of my clothes, and finally take care of my wound. I hiss while ripping the tape from my skin. Standing in front of the bathroom sink, I wash and sterilize the puncture wound in my side. Lucky for me, the blade was small, but it needs stitches. Having done it several times before, I gather the necessary equipment to doctor myself.

With my wound cleaned and sewn, I grab a quick shower to wash away the filthy residue left behind from killing the man behind the trigger that killed Amber. I stare at my reflection in the fogged-up mirror, thinking I'll see a difference in the man staring back at me, not confident that I do. What I look like is tired. The lines on my face appear more defined, as if the past few years have finally caught up with me. I pull in a deep breath, releasing it slowly.

Turning my head, I look across the bedroom at the woman lying in my bed. I acknowledge that something is different. That I feel something when I look at Bea. I haven't felt anything other than anger in a long time, but when she reached out and took my hand, I felt grounded.

I hear a meow at my feet, and I look down. "I bet you're starving." Meowing is the response I get, so I pick it up off the floor and turn off the bathroom light. We head for the kitchen, where I pour a bit of milk on a small plate and place it on the floor with the kitten, who immediately laps it up. I rummage through the cabinets, find a can of tuna, open it, and set the can next to the saucer of milk.

Thirsty myself, I grab a glass. Opening the bottle of whiskey sitting on the counter, I pour myself a drink and stroll into the living room. I toss some logs into the fireplace, start a fire, then sit on the sofa.

The effects of the whiskey and exhaustion soon cause my eyelids to grow heavy.

*Don't be afraid to love again, Foster.*

"Amber?" I mumble, prying my eyes open and glancing around the room, seeing only shadows dancing on the walls, caused by the flames flickering on the burning logs in the fireplace. I shake my head. Maybe I poured a bit too much liquor in my glass tonight.

As I drift off to sleep, I think of the woman in my bed with the bee tattoo whose touch left me wanting something more in my life for the first time in forever.

# 6

# BEATRIX

I wake up warm, snuggled beneath a soft blanket that smells of pine and cedar. Struggling to open my eyes, I bring my knee up to my chest, sinking further into the most comfortable bed I've ever slept in. That thought has my eyes snapping open and me sitting up, suddenly realizing I'm not in my bed. I scan around myself, taking in the large bedroom. To my right is a floor-to-ceiling window with the barest hint of sunshine peeking through the crack in the deep gray curtains. On the opposite side of the bedroom is an oak dresser, and I notice how it matches the nightstands on either side of the king-size bed. And on the floor at the foot of the bed is a large cedar chest. My mind begins to race. I'm in his bed. My body tingles but not in a bad way at the thought of my mysterious savior. I can't believe I asked a stranger to stay in here with me, but I couldn't shake the overwhelming feeling that he would keep me safe. I don't know how to explain it. It's like there was some outside force drawing me toward him. He's intense and scary, yet I'm not scared of him.

Shaking off my crazy thoughts, I shove the blanket aside and swing my legs over the edge of the bed. That's when I spot a bottle of pain reliever with the cap off and a bottle of water sitting on the nightstand. Reaching out, I swipe the bottle, shake out two pills, pop them in my mouth, twist the cap off the water, and eagerly wash down the medicine. My head still hurts, but it's not as bad as before.

Setting the half-empty water bottle back on the table, I struggle to stand and pad over to the en-suite bathroom. I flip the light switch then wince, my eyes unprepared for the brightness. Once my eyes adjust, I take in the sheer size of the bathroom, which is almost the size of the bedroom. It's my dream bathroom. On one side is a walk-in shower that could fit my entire bathroom back home. On the opposite side from the shower is an oversized clawfoot tub. You could easily fit three people in it. "Wow," I mutter.

Making my way over to the sink, I notice a pile of clothes with an unopened toothbrush on top. I peer down to find the filthy garments I've had on for the past couple of days removed, but I don't remember taking them off myself. My face heats. He must have taken my clothes off me.

I stare at my reflection, taking in all the bruises and my swollen face. Russ did a number on me. How can someone be so evil?

I want to wash away every memory of what happened in that basement. Without wasting another moment, I strip while walking over to the shower, open the glass door, and turn on the hot water. It doesn't take long for it to heat, and the second I step under the spray of hot water, I close my eyes and let out a throaty moan.

After I've finished with my shower, I wrap a fluffy towel around my body and make my way over to the sink to brush my teeth. When I pick up the clothes left on the counter, I hold them up. Ghost gave me a pair of men's sweatpants and a plain, long sleeve t-shirt. I'll admit, butterflies erupted inside my tummy at the thought of wearing his clothes. Discarding the towel, I pull on the pants, which are several sizes too big, making me have to roll them at the waist. Thankfully they have a drawstring, or they'd fall off my frame. Next, I slip the shirt over my head, the hem falling to my thighs.

Looking in the mirror, I take in my reflection. I look utterly ridiculous, but I love it because they're his clothes. And just like that, the butterflies are back. With one last glance in the mirror, I take a deep breath. I don't know what awaits me beyond the bedroom walls, but it's time to find out.

A thought creeps into my brain. What if he wants me to leave? Do I want to go back to the bar and my empty life? Waves of sadness and loss overwhelm me at the mere idea of having to do any of those things.

Mustering all my courage, I exit the bathroom and cross to the bedroom door. A savory aroma assaults my senses when I open it, making my stomach rumble and my mouth water. I slowly walk down the hall, my heart rate picking up with each step I take. When I reach the living room, I take in the warmth from the fireplace but no Ghost. Padding around the corner to the kitchen, I find it empty. I do, however, discover the source of the delicious smell simmering on the stovetop.

A faint thwacking draws my attention, and I move toward the direction the sound is coming from, slowly making my way to the living room window. Flicking the curtain back, I peer out, noticing a man off in the distance.

Biting my bottom lip, I decide to step outside. Next to the door, I spot my shoes and slip them on. A gust of cold air hits my face when I step outside, making me shiver. Ignoring the chill, I wrap my arms around my waist as I walk further off the porch and trek toward the man. With each step, my heart rate increases. My breath catches when he swings the ax in his hands. Before he brings it down into the length of wood, his head jerks in my direction, and his intense stare stops me in my tracks. We hold each other's gaze for a moment before he drops the ax to the ground, suddenly eating the distance between us.

"What are you doing out here?" Ghost grunts, the sound of his voice deep and grave. He shrugs off his coat and wraps it around my shoulders. "Arms in." His tone is low, barely audible.

I close my eyes and breathe in his scent. It smells of cedar, smoke, and pine. When I open my eyes, I catch him staring at me and feel my cheeks heat. *What is wrong with me?* Coming to my senses, I force my mouth to form words. "I need to be able to see you." I want to kick myself for being so honest.

"Come on," he says, leading me back to his cabin.

Inside, I follow him into the kitchen. Ghost doesn't speak a word, instead opening the cabinet and pulling down a bowl. He stomps over to the stove, picks up a spoon, scoops out whatever is in the pot and dumps it in the bowl. "Eat." He places the food down on the table. My stomach chooses that moment to let out an audible growl.

I give him a small smile. "Thanks," I whisper. Shrugging off his coat, I hang it over the back of the chair and sit.

My rescuer leans against the counter, crosses his arms over his broad chest, and proceeds to watch me while I eat. I try ignoring the way his eyes burn straight through me. My hands shake when lifting the spoon, and I keep my eyes trained on the bowl of beef soup. I moan as the savory flavors dance across my tongue. A deep growl from Ghost has my head lifting and my eyes connecting with his gray ones. The look on his face is heated. Everything about the man is intense. He is hands-down the most attractive man I have ever laid eyes on. He easily stands around six-foot-four and has brown hair with a generous amount of gray. He looks in his early forties, but the lines around his eyes and the gray in his hair suggest he's possibly older. I can tell from how his biceps stretch the material of his shirt that he works out. But beneath all his handsome features is something more.

"It's time to talk," he grunts.

I swallow past the lump in my throat. "Okay. What do you want to know?"

"You sure you got no one you need to call?"

"I'm sure," I tell him. "I don't have anyone. My dad passed away two years ago, so it's just me."

Ghost's gray eyes study me for a second. "All right, let's start with how you ended up in Mejia's basement."

I scrunch my forehead. "Mejia?" I tuck a strand of my wet hair behind my ear. "You mean, Russ?" I shift in my seat, feeling uneasy under his heavy stare. "I take it Russ isn't his real name?" I look at Ghost, who confirms with a tight nod. I take a deep breath. "He was a regular at the bar where I work. He'd been coming in for over a year."

"How did he snatch you?" he asks through gritted teeth. His obvious irritation makes me nervous, and I do my damnedest to avoid looking at him. "Eyes," he bites out. My head snaps up. "I'm not mad at you, baby." He softens his tone. "I'm angry at the motherfucker for putting his fucking hands on you."

Shocked, I can only stare at Ghost as his words resonate. There is no ignoring that he called me baby or how it made me feel. Clearing my throat, I continue. "Um...anyway, Russ, he uh...liked me. I thought he was harmless. He seemed kind of shy, and I never thought—" My words get stuck in my throat. "He was waiting for me at my house the night he took me. He was at the bar and ordered his usual. He was polite, ate his meal, drank his beer, paid, then left. Just like he always did."

A moment of silence hangs between us before Ghost asks, "Did he..." He leaves his sentence hanging.

I notice his stiff posture and clenching fists and know what he's trying to ask. I shake my head. "No. He didn't get the chance, if that was his intention." I close my eyes and take a deep breath. It's not lost on me what Russ—Mejia—whatever his name is would have done had Ghost not shown up when he did. Remembering the sound of his voice in my ear and the feel of shackles against my skin, my stomach churns.

A large, calloused hand cupping my jaw brings me out of my nightmare. I peer up at him, who is standing in front of me. A single tear slides down my cheek, and he uses the pad of his thumb to wipe it away. "No one will ever hurt you again," Ghost declares, his words delivering a promise and his touch giving me hope.

# 7

# GHOST

Bea looks at me as if I have the answers to all her problems. Like I can give her the moon and stars. Little does she know that when I look at her, I feel the need to provide her with everything she's ever hoped for and more. *Pull your shit together.* I pull my hand back, attempting to break our intense connection.

A tsunami of guilt crashes into me. *What the hell am I doing?* She's vulnerable right now and too fucking fragile. I clench my fists at my sides, my fingernails digging into the flesh of my palms. Then my thoughts shift to Amber, and my mood darkens further. "Eat," I grumble.

Bea's eyes linger on my face for a second longer before dropping to her food as she stirs the contents of her bowl with the spoon. "What's your real name?" she asks.

For a beat, I hesitate to tell her but then decide otherwise. "Foster." Without her looking up at me, I see the corners of her mouth turn up in a small smile.

"I like it, but Ghost seems to suit you better." She lifts a chunk of carrot to her lips and takes a bite. I watch her like a hawk, fixating on minor details of her face. Sunlight through the window highlights her freckles. Her lashes flutter against the apples of her cheeks. "Do you have any family?" she asks.

"Not around here, and my parents and younger brother live out west in Colorado," I answer, finding it easy to share a bit of myself with her.

"Must have been nice growing up with a sibling." Bea continues to eat while memories take me back to my childhood. She looks at me. "You miss them?" I nod. "I can tell." She pauses, then says, "I sense you haven't seen them for a while?" She waits for a reply, but I just stare at her. She's reading me like an open book; admittedly, I don't mind. "Don't take the time you have with them for granted. You can't get back the time lost." She speaks with deep sadness and regret that only someone who has experienced loss and loneliness can have.

She couldn't be closer to the truth if she tried. I haven't seen my family since burying my wife. Not that they haven't tried. I've kept them at a distance for a reason. I never want them tainted by my actions. I already lost one person I loved, and I'm not about to lose any more. If I only have myself, then I'm the only one evil can touch.

I shift my attention after noticing the gray kitten wander across the kitchen floor to Bea's feet and begin swatting at the lace on her shoe. She tears her eyes from my face and looks down at her feet. "Hey there." She smiles and scoops the fuzzy critter up. "You're so soft and adorable." Bea scrubs the kitten's furry face across her cheek. "What's its name?"

"Don't know." I lean against the counter and cross my arms over my chest, thankful for the distraction the little furball is creating.

"How do you not know your own pet's name?" she asks, while the kitten plays with the sleeve of her shirt.

"Not mine. I took him from Mejia's house."

Bea whips her head up to look at me. "You rescued the kitten too?"

There it is—that look she gave me before.

"You shouldn't look at me like that." I feel a gamut of emotions hit my chest like a ton of bricks. I stare at her because I find it hard not to look away.

"Look at you...how am I looking at you?" Bea tilts her head to one side while showing attention to the kitten in her lap.

"Like I'm a good person." I clench my jaw tight. "I am not." If she only knew what I have done and will continue to do.

Bea's eyes fall to her lap while silence closes around us and the air thickens. "Why were you there? At Russ—Mejia's, I mean?" she asks, never taking her eyes off the kitten. "You don't have to answer that question. It's just... well, if you hadn't shown up for whatever reason, you would never have found me." She takes a deep breath. "I'm afraid no one ever would."

She's right. Mejia would have killed her. Like I'm sure many of his victims did, she would have become one of the forgotten. I clench my fists at the mere thought. Keeping distance between us, I decide to tell her the truth. "Four years ago, he killed my wife." Bea lifts her head, and her green eyes connect with mine. She says nothing. She doesn't need to. Her emotions sit on the surface, and I can read her like an open book too. Her eyes are a wide-open window to her soul. She has questions, lots of them, but is keeping them to herself. "He was sent to kill me, but I hadn't returned from another mission. She died when it should have been me," I confess. "So, don't go lookin' at me like I carry all the answers or I'm some kind of hero, because I am far from it." I hold out my rough, calloused hands. "They're unclean. Stained with the blood of lives I have taken." I shake my head. "There is evil in this world, baby... I'm one of them."

"Foster." Bea calls me by my name, and I'm not prepared for

how my name passing through her lips makes me feel. Like a man still worthy of being saved.

"Don't," I bark, and it causes her to shrink into herself. She frowns and looks away. Once again, I close the space between us. Reaching out, I lift her chin. "Let me see you." She faces me again. "I'm sorry. I don't mean to be so harsh." Bea bites her lower lip and my eyes fall to her mouth. I want so badly to kiss her. "Finish your meal." I take a step back, turn, and walk away.

I head for my bedroom and into the bathroom. Reaching the shower, I turn the water on and strip out of my clothes. The bathroom quickly fills with steam before I step into the shower. The hot water cascades over my body, stinging my skin. I rest my palms against the contrasting coldness of the wall tiles and hang my head, closing my eyes as the water pelts against my scalp. *What the fuck is wrong with me?* I've known of this woman's existence for not even 48 hours, and she is all I can think about. She has been through hell, and here I am, wanting her in ways I haven't wanted someone else in a long time.

I suddenly sense I'm no longer alone. "I know you're there, baby." Nothing but silence follows, so I lift my head and glance through the glass enclosure to find Bea standing there in the doorway of the bathroom, fixated on me. I face her fully and slide open the shower door. The hunger in her eyes unleashes my want for her as she drinks me in. She walks toward me, each step closing the gap between us. "I told you; you shouldn't look at me like that, baby," I say, as she stops, leaving a small space between us. "What do you want from me?" I ask with a deep ache in my chest.

"Anything you're willing to give." Her voice is thick with need. She reaches out and touches her palm to my cheek.

"I'm not good for you." I keep my eyes locked on hers.

Bea rises onto her tiptoes, bringing her lips a breath from mine. "You make me feel things I've never felt before, Foster."

"I want to kiss you so badly it hurts," I confess, and cup her face in my hands. "Tell me no," I beg, fearing that once my lips touch hers, I won't be able to catch myself from falling.

"It's ok." Bea stares into the depth of my soul. "I'll catch you."

My mouth crashes against hers. The taste of her kiss is my undoing. I break away long enough to remove the oversized clothes from her body, then pull her into the shower to join me.

"You are beautiful," I tell her, before kissing her again. I shouldn't be doing this. Her hands begin exploring my body, searing every inch of skin her fingertips touch. My hands slip around her waist, sliding over the curves of her hips and pulling her body flush against mine. "This is wrong,"

"We need this," Bea pants, letting out a long moan when I cup one breast and roll her taut nipple between my fingers. "Oh, God." Enjoying her moans, I do the same to her other breast, giving it equal attention. "Help me forget the past couple of days, Foster." She reaches between us, taking my cock in her hand. Her touch causes me to hiss.

I drop to my knees, bringing myself face-level with her pussy. "I need to taste you." I look up at her and she nods, threading her fingers through my hair. I grip her ass in my palms and pull her closer, dipping between her thighs. The taste of her pussy explodes in my mouth as I run my tongue through her slit. Her hips buck forward, and her passionate moans fuel my need to make her mine. I suck and lap at her swollen clit until her legs begin to quiver. Knowing she's close, I stop and stand, and Bea moans in protest. I kiss her with the taste of her pussy on my lips. "As much as I love the taste of your pussy, baby, I want you to come on my dick more." I guide us out of the shower and to the bed. Dripping wet, I lay her down and settle between her legs. I gaze down at her, my cock waiting at her entrance.

She lifts her hand to my cheek. "I'm with you, Foster. Let go."

8

# BEATRIX

My skin prickles when Foster's teeth nip at my neck, causing my breath to catch. A moan escapes my lips when he grinds his hips, sinking his cock farther inside me. My eyes roll to the back of my head when he drops his arm, and his large hand grabs a handful of my flesh, lifting my ass, the movement causing the head of his cock to bump against my cervix.

"Fuck," he grunts.

"Foster," I moan, moving my legs around his waist. Though he's as deep as he can go, it doesn't feel as if it is enough. His body engulfs me, his cock inside me, and his lips on mine don't feel like enough. He keeps me on edge—my release is right here—but the painfully slow rhythm of him gliding in and out of me is the sweetest torture.

Sensing I need more, Foster pulls out and flips to his back, bringing me to straddle him. "Ride me," he demands, grabbing my hips in a bruising grip.

Settling my palms against his chest, I allow him to guide the tip of his cock to my entrance and slowly lower myself. The

46

moment I'm fully seated, my pussy spasms, and I moan at the feeling of being so full.

I watch him grit his teeth and his jaw tick. The cords of his neck strain as he gazes up at me. Finally, his hands leave my hips and his palms skim up my sides until my breasts are encased in his large, callused hands. "Ride me," he repeats.

Giving in to his demand, I begin to move. A growl rumbles in his ribcage when my fingernails dig into his chest. His hands abandon my breasts and latch onto the globes of my ass, urging me to move faster. Soon the room fills with the sounds of his heavy breathing and my moans. My gaze never leaves him, and I love how his eyes drink in every inch of me as I ride him. I watch as his eyes follow the sway of my breasts as I bounce up and down on his cock, then the fire in those grey eyes intensifies as he zeroes in between my thighs where we're connected.

"I'm close," I breathe.

"I can feel it," Foster growls. "Be a good girl and touch your clit."

I lean back, bracing one hand on his thigh while using the other to play with my clit. In this position, I'm entirely open to him.

"That's it. Play with that pretty pussy."

His dirty words only excite me more.

"Fuck," he grunts, when my walls begin to flutter. A moment later, my orgasm crashes through me, my pussy clamps down on him like a vise, and I can feel my release soaking his cock. I scream his name. *"Foster!"*

I barely have time to recover from my orgasm when I find myself on my back, and the air is pushed from my lungs when he begins fucking me. What started soft and sweet becomes animalistic, leaving me no choice but to hold on. He holds me tight as he groans between grunts, driving in repeatedly. I spread my legs wider, accepting all that he's giving me. Reaching between our bodies, he tweaks my clit. I didn't think it was possible, but heat floods my core when his thumb starts stroking me. "I'm coming again," I gasp.

"Come," he orders, burying his face in the crook of my neck and grinding his cock deeper, causing white flashes of light to fill my vision as another orgasm ripples through my body simultaneously. Foster stills and fills me with his release.

The two of us lie wrapped in each other's embrace, neither making a move to separate as we catch our breath. I welcome the heavy weight of Foster's frame like a warm blanket and run my fingers through his hair. I smile when I feel his lips brush against the sensitive spot behind my ear.

"Come shower with me." He nips my ear, making me giggle.

"Okay." I sigh at the loss when he pulls out of me, but I don't lose his heat for long before he winds his arm around my waist and tugs me out of bed with him. Not used to having my naked body on such display, I tamp down the urge to cover myself. On the other hand, he is entirely comfortable with his nakedness, as he should be. As we make our way into the bathroom, I take a moment to admire all he is: tall, with broad shoulders, lean hips, and muscular thighs. And nearly every inch of his arms and back are covered in colorful ink.

Pausing briefly at the large walk-in shower, Foster reaches into the stall and turns the water on. Not letting go of my hand, he guides us inside. He doesn't speak as he picks up a bottle, squeezes some shampoo into his palm, then begins massaging my scalp. He washes my hair with a gentleness you wouldn't expect from a man like him. Something has changed within him since this morning. It's almost as if a weight has been lifted off his shoulders. I see it in his eyes. At this moment, I realize I, too, feel different.

I feel at peace for the first time in a long time. *Is Foster my missing puzzle piece? Is he the one my soul has been searching for?*

As this newfound clarity comes to light, I let out a shaky exhale. I don't even realize I have a death grip on Foster's biceps until he speaks.

"Are you okay?"

At the sound of his deep voice, I open my eyes and see his face marred with worry. "I feel at home here. I don't feel lost anymore." My voice shakes as I choke on my confession and lock eyes with his. "I don't want to go back to my life." Tears start pouring down my face. "I want to stay here with you." I cling to Foster as my body begins to tremble. The thought of returning to my dead, empty life fills me with unease.

Taking my face between the palms of his large hands, Foster fixes his intense eyes on me. "You feel at home because you are home and don't belong anywhere but with me."

"Are...are you saying I can stay? I can stay here with you?" I hiccup.

"I'm not sure I'd give you a choice in the matter," he grinds out, his voice turning hard. "I'm not letting you go, baby." He kisses me hard. "Do you fucking understand what I'm saying?"

I nod, relief washing over me. "Yes."

---

Early the following day, we pull into the bar's parking lot. As we lay in bed last night, I told him about Sully and how he was a friend of my father's, that he has been like an uncle to me, and how I worked for him for the past several years.

Foster pulls into a parking spot and cuts the engine. "You sure you don't want to hang around so you can talk to him in person?"

I shake my head. "This is the way he would have wanted it. The man said the same thing to me every day after my father passed." I turn in my seat and look at him. "He always said he hoped he would arrive to work one day, and I wouldn't be here. All he ever wanted was for me to leave this place and find what makes me happy." I turn back and peer through the passenger window, fogging up from the cold. "I felt lost for so long. I don't know why I never took Sullivan's advice just to leave. To go somewhere, anywhere, else. It's like he knew I was dead inside. Like a part of me was eaten away by the cancer that stole my dad from me."

I turn back to Foster. "I know now that the universe had another plan for me—you." He reaches across the seat and grips the back of my neck, pulling me in for a brutal kiss. "I don't understand how one of the worst moments of my life leads to one of the best," I tell him. "But I'm thankful it did.".

"If I could, I would bring that sorry piece of shit back to life, thank him for giving you to me, then slowly watch as his soul left this earth as I sank my blade into his heart until every drop of blood drained from his body."

After another bruising kiss, Foster releases me from his hold, and I open the truck door. The cold wind nips at my skin, making me shiver. Taking the piece of paper and thumb tack from my pocket, I make my way up to the bar's entrance.

I look down at the folded letter and close my eyes. When I open them, I peer over my shoulder at Foster, now standing at the truck's hood, arms folded across his chest and his eyes on me. I give him a small smile, then turn back, kiss the letter, and tack it to the door.


*Sullivan,*
  *I did it.*
  *Love always,*
  *Beatrix*


**The End is just the beginning**

CRYSTAL DANIELS
Two Pens
One Story
SANDY ALVAREZ